The Meeting of the

Seeker of the Songs Book 1

By Matthew Warren

Life Choices and Friends

Maddy sighed as she leaned against an apple tree on the side of the road leading to Neverwinter, her home. She considered the path in life she had chosen, the life of a bard. Unlike most bards, she was a master of neither harp or flute. Nor was she greatly skilled at performing magic or illusions.

The citizens of Faerun did enjoy her, however; for her acrobatics, her verses, her tales, and, (Maddy's favorite thing to do), singing. Many of the dwarves in Neverwinter looked forward to her visits, as she was well versed in dwarven drinking songs, heroic tales, and, most importantly to them, she was able to keep up in dwarven drinking games.

A length of her lilac-colored hair caught her attention, bringing her out of her deep thoughts. Pulling back her hood, she let her long hair out and inspected herself. Her hair, while lightly colored like the purple flower, was so faint that most passed it over, thinking she was blonde. Her face was gentle and most could not tell her sex from it. Her skin was pale, with hints of red that most believed to be from traveling on sunny days. She was almost as tall as most human males. If not for her scarlet and yellow checkered cloak, she would be mistaken for a young farmhand. Her leather armor top was made specifically to hide her female figure. It was not safe for a woman to travel the roads unescorted, but Maddy could handle most trouble.

Trouble had been what brought her to this apple tree, now that she thought of it.

    ** *She was just minding her own business, drinking away the time between performances, when she was approached. Three ugly brutes looking for gold invited her to a game of cards, hoping to take her hard earned coin. After ten gambits of three dragon ante, the brutes had lost a total of 150 coppers. They were not pleased about losing and to pacify them she bought them each a glass of good strong wine.*

Knowing her time there was done, she got up to leave. One of the brutes grabbed after her and pulled back her hood, trying to get her to stay. Her face and long hair were enough for these men to realize that they had been beaten at cards by a woman. They were greatly angered and drew their swords- they would not let their reputation at cards be ruined by being beaten by a human female. Maddy had quickly tugged her hood away from the leader of the brutes, kicked him swiftly between the legs, and ran for it. As she ran for the door, the innkeeper tossed Maddy her pack and walking staff. Blowing a kiss to the inn keeper, Maddy made great haste to the road.**

A spike of pain drew her thoughts away from her latest adventure. She pulled her cloak away from her body to look at her broken leg. Reaching into her top, she removed a strip of leather tied around a silver coin. On the front of the coin was the profile of a woman smiling with long hair. As is the ritual of her faith she kissed the coin and gave thanks to her goddess Tymora. Tymora was the Goddess of luck, and many travelers, gamblers, and especially Bards worshipped her. Even followers of other deities gave tribute to her church, hoping for her blessing. It had been luck that she received this broken leg and for that she thanked Tymora.

** The brutes, whom were terrible at cards, had chased after her, forcing her to choose between them or jumping off the bridge into the raging river several feet below. The brutes licked their lips and Maddy got a shiver thinking what horrible plans they had. She had heard of bandits and thugs doing horrible things to women in the wilderness. The river creaked as ice panels broke off and floated down the river. Maddy decided that the best action was the unexpected, and dived into the freezing waters below. Her last memory before waking up on the river shore was hitting the bottom of the deep water, where there was a rock, and passing out from the pain as her leg broke. **

She smiled; Tymora had blessed her for her courage, for she limped away with her life at the fair price of a broken leg. The brutes left her for dead, which in itself was good luck as most of the time people loot the dead. She loved the Goddess of Luck, no matter what kind of luck she had.

Suddenly the branches of the tree she was laying against swayed as if from wind. A ripe apple snapped off of its branch and fell down towards her. Without looking up, Maddy put her hand out. Several seconds passed and she blinked. Her ice-blue eyes darted all around her, but the apple she swore she had heard falling was nowhere to be seen. Maybe it was her Goddess playing games with her, but she had no time to ponder this, for that was when she heard the churning of wagon wheels coming from behind her. The telltale clunk of someone landing in the wagon spiked Maddy's nerves- usually she was better at sensing hidden people.

The wagon had stopped just on the other side of the tree. Pressing herself closer to the tree, she listened intently. "Thank you, dear Asuka, I was getting a little tired of eating salted meat," stated an airy, musical voice. There was a silence, "Asuka, do not despair. Your salted meats are wonderful; it is just nice to taste something sweet." With that there was a crunch of an apple. Maddy's stomach rumbled; she had rested under the tree hoping to eat one. "Is there something more, my dear? If not, please sit," suggested the voice.

Another voice spoke, who Maddy assumed was Asuka: "Mistress, there is a person on the other side of the tree. It would not bother me, but I heard labored breathing, though they tried to suppress it. I believe the person is hiding, and is in pain."

Maddy eyes grew big. She thought to herself, "That must have been the noise, this Asuka person was in the tree above me."

"Such a good girl you are, Asuka. You are right, we should see to this poor soul." Maddy heard the two of them coming around the tree on foot. She looked up and saw before her two females. One was wearing a dark green silk robe and had reddish-blonde hair. She was holding a wooden staff, and looking Maddy over searchingly, with eyes deep and blue as a lake.

The other had auburn skin, amber eyes, and chestnut hair. She was wearing hides and carried a sharp spear, which she clutched defensively.

Odd runes, only visible to Maddy, danced above their heads. Maddy could tell from the runes that they were good people, and let out a sigh as she relaxed.

"Well now, I see why you were stumped. Tell us, human; are you a girl or a boy?" the red hair woman asked as her eyes moved back and forth as she questioned Maddy. Maddy got the distinct feeling she was searching for Maddy's wounds.

Maddy smirked and caustically stated, "By the Goddess of this world, I am very much who I choose to be." Maddy let out a grunt of pain as she sat up straighter. "However, if it will get me passage on your wagon, and enable me to take off this infernal chest piece, then I will admit I was born female." Maddy reached behind herself and unbuckled her leather chest plate to reveal her blue tunic and the prominent mounds underneath." I am called Maddy. As well I am a bard. Who will I thank my Goddess Tymora for sending?"

"I," Began the woman with the reddish-gold hair, "am Sister Ranaa. And this," she gestured towards the woman with the spear, "is my precious, Asuka." The woman with the spear bowed, but kept her eyes in contact with Maddy's.

Kneeling before Maddy, Sister Ranaa pulled back Maddy's cloak and found the splint that she had tied around her broken leg.

"Foolish girl, you could have gotten an infection from walking on this leg and lying in the dirt." After scolding her, Sister Ranaa hummed softly. As she touched Maddy's leg and removed the splint, it became fully healed.

Slowly, Maddy walked around on her leg. She had been healed before, but this did not even hurt a little. Elegantly, Maddy bowed before Sister Ranaa, and said, "I have not the money to repay you, but perhaps you will take my stories as we head to the next village. I will repay you in kind with room and board. Now that I am able to walk, I am sure the good innkeepers will allow me to perform."

Asuka's eyes lit up and she looked towards Sister Ranaa. Sister Ranaa nodded her head. "Tell me Maddy, did your Goddess bless you with a singing voice? We would love to hear some local songs, instead of stories."

Maddy bowed with a whisk of her cape, "I can sing in a high chant, or that of a sweet maiden." Maddy took a seat on the wagon next to Sister Ranaa, while Asuka laid down in the back resting.

Maddy began singing, not a lyrics but a melodious tune. Sister Ranaa thought to herself how the sun shone brighter, but it suddenly seemed more pleasantly mild in temperature.

Deals, Bargains, and Hard Cider

Maddy smiled as they began crossing over the Sleeping Dragon. A marvel of the city of Neverwinter, the bridge was carved delicately into the form of its namesake. She was finally here, and almost on time. Being chased by the bandits and breaking her leg had cost her valuable time. Luckily. joining Sister Ranaa and Asuka helped get Maddy to Neverwinter on time.

Turning to her two new friends, Maddy grinned wolfishly and proclaimed, "Welcome to Neverwinter, my friends! Now, if you will please bear with me..." Maddy leapt into a standing position. She then balanced on one foot, and called out in a booming voice. "Ladies and Gentlemen, I will be performing feats, singing, and telling tales at the Merry Willow inn tonight! Come one, come all!"

As Maddy finished she performed a back flip and landed in a single-handed handstand. A few peasants clapped, but most just went about their daily lives carrying barrels and wheat to be sold at the market.

"Your reputation does not seem to precede you, child?" suggested Sister Ranaa in a pitying tone. She paid close attention to the peasants passing on her sides, wanting to be sure not to run them over with the wagon wheels.

Maddy, without her smile fading in the slightest, replied under her breath, "Sadly, no, most of these people are sexist. They believe women should perform nothing but private dances." When Ranaa gave her a quizzical look at the mention of private dances, Maddy merely sniffed distastefully to discourage curiosity.

As they passed through the market area, Asuka took careful note as to where salted meats and furs where being traded and sold. Maddy looked for fruit stands. She was hoping apples were available, and, even more so, hard cider. Sister Ranaa smiled when saw a fruit-stand selling strawberries.

They were all hungry, and tired after their journey here. They were ready for the warm bed and meal Maddy had promised them. A sign swung softly ahead of them. On it was a picture of a willow with the wind blowing in its branches. A closer inspection revealed there was a kindly old woman's smiling face carved on the willow.

"Let me go inside and inform the innkeeper of our arrival, while you take the horse and wagon to the stables," Maddy said, backflipping three times to the door and bowed with a flourish of her cape. A group of peasants walked into the inn after her.

"I have come to perform at your inn tonight. I will be requiring a large room with privacy for me and my guests. I will also be requesting supper and breakfast the next morning."

Huffing, the dwarf innkeeper looked up from his booking log, and gave Maddy a glare to be reckoned with. "You will be paying for your drinks this time, and I will not hear otherwise. You are late. You will be held responsible for it."

Maddy began to open her mouth, when the innkeeper spoke up again. "Do not give me excuses, lass! You're lucky I let you perform at all. Your mother is furious. You know full well any trouble you got yourself into was rightly earned." With this the innkeeper rubbed his balding head and stroked his fine iron-black beard. "Also, if you plan to perform here tonight, you best be singing my favorite song."

He crossed his arms, and puffed smoke from his pipe, waiting for Maddy's reply. Maddy's cheeks were spotted with color. It had been a while since she was talked to in such away. She felt like a child again. Bowing her head she said sullenly, "Yes, sir. Thank you for allowing me to keep my position." Maddy leaned in close so that no one could hear or see. She kissed the dwarf's cheek and whispered, "Thank you Papa, love you." Quickly she whisked herself away.

Maddy then helped Asuka with the boxes of furs and salted meats. When Asuka walked into the inn carrying a box of her salted boar, the innkeeper barked, "You there, with the box, come here!" Asuka walked over to the dwarf, who sniffed the box. "That is fine-smelling boar you have there, lass. I need to restock my kitchen. I am sure I can offer you a nice bit of coin for it, much better than those vultures they call merchants here." Asuka stood there, stunned into silence, until Maddy came in.

"Asuka, this is Rooter Rockhide, the innkeeper," Maddy announced. The wild elf girl relaxed and bowed, still holding the box.

"Ahhh, so you're one of Maddy's traveling companions, then. I will make you a deal: top coin, and your drinks are on the house." Maddy smiled as Rockhide said this, but Rockhide quickly added. "Not yours though, girly. You're still paying."

Sighing, Maddy left as Sister Ranaa came in, and took her place next to Asuka. Finally speaking, Asuka turned to Sister Ranaa and informed her of the situation. Rockhide invited Sister Ranaa and Asuka to sit and deal over the table. Rockhide called for drinks and told Maddy to finish unpacking. He told Maddy she would earn one free hard apple cider when she finished.

An hour later, exhausted, Maddy joined them at the table. They were all grinning. Sister Ranaa and Asuka were picking at a nice meat pie. Rooter Rockhide slid a sizable pouch of silver coins over to them. As Maddy sat down, a lovely elven woman, with hair that looked spun from gold, laid a stein of cold hard apple cider in front of Maddy and leaned over. "My dear, we have much to talk about. I expect you to perform your best." Maddy, without looking at the woman, nodded, and kissed her hand softly. The elven woman strode off smiling.

The dwarf grinned wide, for it had been too long since the elven woman had been to his inn. "Saffera is performing tonight at the town center. I cannot leave my inn to see her, but at least our daughter is here to entertain us instead. Saffera will have the next two nights off, with the money she will make tonight. We should all be lucky to have dinner as a family." To this Maddy respectfully kissed her silver coin. The dwarf smiled again.

A Night In the Life of a Bard…Maddy's Tale:

After their meal of hard ciders and boar stew with roots, Mathus, the inn's cook, came to the table with an apple pie. Maddy smiled and thanked him as he placed a slice for her on a fresh clean plate. After serving the others Mathus bowed his head and returned to the kitchen. Ranaa enjoyed the pie, eating it slowly, while Asuka ate hers with her hands, licking the sweet filling off her fingers.

Rockhide closed his log and watched the fires of the main room die out. It was now late and most of the patrons have gone to their rooms. Maddy was in a corner with a few sturdier patrons who were enjoying off-key drinking songs. Rockhide had been the one to teach Maddy all the best dwarfish drinking songs. This was the way they operated; Maddy would encourage the richer patrons to stay up to sing of good times, while getting them to buy more and more of her father's ales and ciders. Two of the patrons had recently stumbled to their nicer chambers after dropping gold coins on the table.

Mathus was popping in and out of his kitchen to bring more drinks, as the wenches were doing the dishes or had gone to sleep. Rockhide lightly tapped his stone carved pipe to remove the ashes. He himself was ready for bed and had enjoyed listening to the story of how Torm ascended to Godhood.

Suddenly there was a knock at the door. Rockhide bolted up surprised and then slapped his forehead. He had locked up the door, having forgotten that Maddy's new friends had not yet come back. Going quickly, he grabbed a silver key out of his pouch and unlocked the door. Without thinking, Rockhide rolled backwards and out of the way of a great ax.

Howling evilly, a dark furry figure entered, swinging its axe once again at the innkeeper. However, this time Rockhide was ready. He dodged again and kicked the dark creature hard in the back of the knee. The patrons, hearing the crash as the monster fell to the ground, got out of their seats quickly and stumbled to their rooms as fast as their feet could take them.

As the first of the fiends was getting up another kicked the door open wide. There was a flash of red light which told those still in the room that some of the city was on fire. The creature raised a wickedly jagged sword above its head, letting out a guttural cry. Without warning, the creature dropped its sword, raking at its back, and slammed into the first fiend, pinning the other with its dead body. Sticking out of the horrible beast were the shafts of three arrows.Rockhide, being an old warrior, admired the precision of the shots.

Looking up he saw a tall, wild elf with dark hair. Stepping on top of the creature she'd killed, she drew her bow and silenced the other, pinned fiend with an arrow through its throat. "Good to see you are well, Master Rockhide," remarked the elf, who he now remembered was named Asuka. Together they gazed upon the fiends of which had attacked them. They had thick black fur and were over two meters high. They had long nails, but not claws, and tusk-like teeth jutting out of their lower jaws. Their eyes, even glazed with death, were pure black.

"What do you believe it is?"Rockhide, coming back to reality, cleared his throat. "It looks like a really furry orc to me. I am glad to see you are okay, but where is Sister Ranaa?" He asked, puzzled by it all.

"Some of the guards have already evacuated the young and injured. Mistress sent me to see that you made it out and went with the guards to see to the injured."

Rockhide nodded happily. "It is good of your Mistress to so readily go to helping, and good that she sent you. However, my patrons are not in the capacity to leave the city: we must hold the fort."

A sudden rustle gave the dwarf and wild elf rise, but their nerves were quickly settled when Maddy popped her head above the overturned table. "What is going on here? I was having a ...hic...drink and suddenly everyone pushes me over?" Getting to her feet she gave a disgusted look to the dead creatures on the ground. "Oooooh, Mom is going to be...hic...red eyed when she sees you made a mess." Maddy jested with a giggle.

Laughing, Rockhide shook his head. His daughter was the type to rarely be phased by, and even make snarky remarks in, serious situations. It was a very popular issue with bards. Before he could open his mouth again to tell her to stop, there was a sudden crash as the kitchen door flew open and another one of the creatures hit the ground bloodied and dead.

Coming from the doorway was a very pissed Mathus holding what looked like a giant wooden spoon recently coated with disgusting black ichor. "Little sod was eating the honey cakes I had made for my sweet sister's welcome home breakfast." Maddy's usual calm self went white in the face. It was one thing for her to see dead monsters, but to know that she wasn't getting honey cakes in the morning was too much.

"Not the honey cakes...hic...whyyyyyy! Warm tears began to cover her face as she cried over the loss.

"You two stop your silliness and get out there and take care of the town," barked Rockhide. Mathus nodded and ran out the door with a cry of anger toward anyone who would assault his wonderful home. Maddy wavered a bit, wiped off her face, and nodded.

"Maddy, there are a few buildings on fire, you know what to do. Meet your mom at the high tower." She saluted her father and ran off. "I hope you do not mind fighting with an old dwarf, my fair lady Asuka." To this Asuka grinned and notched another arrow, ready to fight tooth and nail.

Maddy ran through the town carrying her bag and a walking staff. Suddenly, she heard a young girl scream. Moving as fast as she could, Maddy turned the corner as one of the furry orc-like creatures began to run off with a small child. Making chase, she swung back her staff and tossed it like a spear. The staff flew true and struck the beast bluntly in the back, causing it to turn around and snarl, gnashing its teeth. Angered, the monster tossed the girl aside and Maddy barely caught her, slamming hard onto the ground with her back.

Wincing, Maddy got up and shooed the girl away, but dropped her guard, getting bitten on the shoulder by jagged teeth that slid into the flesh like shards of stone. Crying out, Maddy used her other arm to punch the break the creature's nose. Her shoulder, now seeping blood, took away the only enjoyable part of being slightly drunk. The creature, backing up, howled and lunged again at Maddy, this time aiming for her throat. Maddy fell backwards and put her foot up to toss the furry orc with its own strength. As the monster smashed face first into the stone wall behind them, dead or just knocked out, Maddy let out a scream. She had thoughtlessly used both her just recently healed leg and her bloodied shoulder, and was now in a world of pain and self loathing.

Coming back to her senses, Maddy tore away the only scrap of her tunic that still covered the shoulder. She ripped a strip off of the bottom of her tunic and made a tourniquet to stop the bleeding. Concentrating through the burning pains she was able to heal the wounds with the little bit of divine magic she knew. While the wound was no longer bleeding there was a tinge of greenness around the remaining teeth marks. She rolled her eyes in annoyance; she knew an infection when she saw one.

Hearing footsteps, she quickly spun around to find a man scribbling on a piece of paper. Her mind screamed at the very idea. People were running for their lives, buildings were burning, and this man was walking around writing.

"You there, what is your name, or what would you like to be known as?" Asked the man as he scratched away at the paper.

"Are you driven by entropy? Get to the evacuation zone with this child!" Commanded Maddy as she gave the child to the man and ran off with her staff before he could ask another question. It had not ocurred to Maddy until she was within a block of the tower that leaving the child with such a man might have been a bad idea. However, she shook off the feeling. The symbols above his head told her that he was trustworthy. She also blushed as she admitted to herself that for a scholar (if he was one), he was actually fairly cute.

The man looked at the child and shrugged. "I got enough here, I guess I should help. Come with me, the guards earlier were shouting about heading to the south." Looking down he saw the little girl raising her hand. "Of course, how silly of me." The scholar took the small girls hand and she smiled as they walked towards the south. "My name is Ryan Slumber, how shall I address my fair little princess?"

Blushing, the little girl buried her face in Ryan's cloak and replied quietly, "I am Bribri. And that was Madelyn Melody, but if you want to be on her good side you should just call her Maddy."

Fever Dreams and Unpleasant Reality

***A young girl with lilac hair was floating in blackness. Her pale skin was a stark contrast to her surroundings. Her blue eyes almost glowed with fierceness. She screamed into the darkness "But why do I have to leave?"

A deep cold voice sending chills through her spine replied, "I told you, Madelyn, you deserve a better life."

"But, I love it here, the ice is so beautiful." As she spoke this, the surrounding darkness gave way to reflective dark blue crystals. She basked in the glow and felt their soothing coolness.

"Madelyn, listen to your father. You want to be a bard, don't you?" In the refection of the ice crystals appeared a woman with bronze hair wearing a heavy cloak. Her eyes were as blue as Madelyn's but her skin was of someone who had been in the sun. Madelyn lowered her eyes to the ground, and rubbed the toe of her shoes in the dirt.

"Why can I not learn from you, Mommy?" Her eyes came up pleadingly.

Madelyn's mother shook her head dismissively. "I have told you. You have to apprentice a Master. Saffera taught me and she has graciously accepted to teach you and take you in." Looking towards the darkness she smiled. "Despite the nature of your father."

The world shattered before the girl as she whimpered. Her world flashed into blinding white light and she found herself holding her harp and hitting a sharp note. In frustration she threw the harp down. "I told you, I do not like the harp. It is too feminine."

Leaning down to pick it up Saffera gave her a stern look, "Madelyn Melody, I have told you the harp is important to learn." She brushed the dust off of the instrument, and offered it back to Madelyn.

Madelyn looked at her with discontent but took it back. "Why can't I just sing and tell stories?" She began humming as though to prove a point.

Patting her head, Saffera said softly, "When a wizard learns their craft they must do hand exercises before they can even begin to learn to read arcane tomes..."

With a heavy sigh Madelyn finished, "A bard must learn to play an instrument before she can begin to sing the song." Nodding reluctantly she again began plucking at the strings. Suddenly, without warning she was struck in the head with a rock. Crying out she raised her hand to her temple and found that it was bleeding. The boys shouted with jeering words about not pretending to be a boy.

She was now in the temple of Torm. The walls were decorated with lovely stained-glass windows. Some held the banner of Torm, an open-palmed, gauntleted hand. Madelyn remembered that Torm was a divine God of law and good. Her new father, Rockhide, was a paladin during a war. It was the God he had chosen to worship and so he brought his daughter to be healed by the priest there.

The cleric at the altar looked at the deep gash on her head that was leaking still with fresh blood. Madelyn did not listen to their whispers, her mind too busy recalling all the stories Rockhide told her of Torm. As far as the Gods were concerned, in this world Torm seemed rather decent, but she liked her new mother's better. Tymora *was far more interesting, a twin goddess who controlled the good side of luck.*

Her thoughts were suddenly halted by the searing pain in her temples as the priest healed her. As always she bit at her tongue to hold back the cries of pain. Now, as she was leaving the shrine, she was allowed to cry. Rockhide patted her lilac hair to comfort her. "One day, dear, you will understand why it hurts when they heal you." Rockhide said, as he always did after a healing. ***

There was a voice in the distance, one she did not remember, and her world shattered again. She bolted up and realized that her forehead was bleeding and it hurt badly. Only this time, a cry came from her bedside. "Son of a monk!" Grasping his head was a familiar fellow that she could not quite place. He used his hands to push himself up and sat in the chair next to her bed, crying out "Is your head made from iron ore, woman?!" as he wiped the blood from the small gash on his forehead.

She looked around to find that she was in her room at the Merry Willow. The soft sheets that Saffera had sewn were clinging to her body. The bed was firm as stone, but that was how she liked it. She spent most her life traveling, so there was no point for a soft bed. There was charcoal in her fireplace, which was a first for her. She liked it cool, and did not even own a blanket. The pillows on her bed pulled her attention suddenly. They were embroidered with a silvery moon in a dark sky. Then her attention shifted to her shoulder. It was bandaged up and stained green with strong smelling herbs. The man had been silently watching over her while she came to. It dawned on her that she was topless, and her breasts where exposed to this stranger. "Who are you? And why are you in my room? Are you a pervert?" Maddy shouted these questions while she covered herself with the soft sheets.

The man sat up straight and diverted his eyes, "My name is Ryan." With a sniff of distaste he added, "I am not a pervert. As for why I am in your room, I wanted to tell you that the girl found her sister and said that she would take her to their mother."

Maddy's head buzzed. "What are you talking about?" she snapped.

Ryan tilted his head to the side, "The village was attacked three nights ago, and you saved a little girl. Then you apparently rang the bell in the tower." Leaning close he looked into her eyes, "And you either do not remember because you slept so long, or because of the fever that could have killed you. Especially in that freak rain storm that night."

"Be that as it may!" Maddy grabbed his collar, and said with anger seething from her words, "What kind of man goes into a woman's room while she sleeps?"

Ryan pulled the bandage wrap from his pockets, "They sent me up to change your bandages and check your temperature." Ryan placed the back of his hand softly on her forehead. When he pulled back, his hand was shaking. "The fever must have broken, you were burning last we checked." Ryan rubbed the back of his hand on her forehead, which had for some reason become very cold, as if someone had snuck in and applied the freezing snow from outside to her brow.

From the wooden dresser next to her bed, Ryan grabbed the wash cloth and pail of warm water. He raised them to her, as if asking permission to wash the herbs from her shoulder. Maddy laid back, growling slightly and holding the sheets tightly against her body. He removed the bandages and threw them into a basket on the floor, then began softly washing her shoulder with the warm water and the cloth. "You spoke in your sleep, perhaps it was a fever dream?" Ryan looked at her, puzzled. "I was raised by scholars in the temples a good distance from here. So I understand not having your parents raise you."

Maddy grabbed his hand roughly and looked into his eyes, "Do not dare to try to console me! You can't begin to think that you can understand my troubles!" She let go and turned her face away from him toward the wall. Her eyes met with the window and out of it she saw clear blue skies. Well, for normal people it would be wonderful, she mused. She had always preferred gray skies or foggy mornings, when the dew drips from the flowers as though still caught in a silent rain.

The warm water on her shoulder gave her a pleasant feeling. It felt very refreshing, though for others it might have been uncomfortable.

Looking at her shoulder while softly touching it to watch the pigment turn from pinkish back to a pale white, Ryan thought to himself that she was rather lovely despite her sudden attitude. He mused about how, when they're not being heroic, people are just people.

He took a fresh cloth, dried her shoulder, and nodded. "The green tint is gone and your fever has broken. You are most likely able to get going." Ryan said as he got up and headed for the door. "Get dressed and be ready for a quick meal. Sister Ranaa urges quickness, something about having to get on their way and taking you with them." Shutting the door behind him, he did not hear Maddy questioning why.

Getting out of bed slowly, to make sure that Ryan did not suddenly come back and catch her exposed, she opened the dresser. She pulled out a pair of cotton undergarments and put them on carefully. Next she grabbed her linen slacks, which were dyed an emerald green. She loved the color green, despite the fact that people believed it contrasted poorly with her lilac hair. She grabbed the soft brown cord she used as a belt and tightened her slacks around her. Looking through the next dresser drawer she picked out a soft cotton blouse that was black with silvery accents. Everyone in town knew she was a girl, so she had no trouble wearing a pretty top here. Looking down at herself, she smiled and held the blouse close to her. The cool cotton felt nice against her skin, much better than her burlap cloak or leather chest piece.

Grabbing her large travel pack, she filled it with what she would need for the next few days. She did not know why Sister Ranaa wanted her to come with them, but she knew she would enjoy the company, so why not.

Maddy moved swiftly across the floor, hardly aware that she was purposefully missing all the boards that creaked when you stepped on them. She had worked very hard in the past to sneak down the stairs so as not to wake Saffera, Mathus, or Rockhide when she would go to the kitchen. She grinned because Mathus knew her so well that before closing the kitchen he would leave a plate with a honey cake and small glass of milk out for her. Her brother was always so good to her.

Like her, Mathus was adopted into the family, only by different means. Rockhide had caught him in the kitchen late one night. He was mixing rice with broth, meat, and vegetables in a large pot. Rockhide watched him from behind the door, unsure as to what he was doing. Instead of fleeing with the food, he grabbed a bowl and sat down to eat, leaving the pot on the counter as though for others.

After Mathus had taken his third bite, Rockhide opened the door and confronted the now scared boy. Grabbing a bowl, Rockhide served himself some of the food. He looked at it, noticing the boy had cooked away the broth to the point that it was not longer a soup. Spooning some up, he sniffed the food and ate a bit. There boar meat had a richness to it, and the vegetables had apparently been cooked with butter and were now soft and flavorful. The rice was pillow soft and sweetened by tomato and chicken. Rockhide continued to eat quietly with the young Mathus.

When they had finished their food Rockhide had taken Mathus to a bedroom and told him he could stay, as long as he cooked, and enjoyed himself while doing so. Mathus had been working there for two months and was considered by many to be Rockhide's son, when Maddy -at that time called Madelyn Melody- and Saffera came to perform. It had been Mathus who, unable to say her name right, had referred to her as Maddy because of her silliness. Maddy had instantly loved the new name. Saffera, over the week of performing at the Merry Willow, had fallen in love with the innkeeper, and they had gotten married. Weeks became months, and before Saffera set off to continue her career they had grown into a very happy family. It had also been Mathus who had ignited Maddy's fondness for apples when he offered them as a topping for her honey cake. A voice stirred her from her memories and she shook her head.

A tall elven woman with reddish-gold hair and skin the color of alabaster was standing before her. Her dark green silk robe did not hang on her, but rather flowed over her like a fine layer of hair. Her lips, a soft pink despite being unpainted, were moving now.

"....Maddy are you paying attention to me? We need to get moving." Ranaa's voice was etched with urgency, and Maddy again shook her head.

"I'm sorry, I am a bit foggy right now, and why do we have to leave?" Maddy looked around and saw that Ryan and Asuka were moving crates toward the door leading to the stables. She wondered why Ryan was helping.

She looked across the tables filled with patrons consuming their lunches and shouting with cheer. Her eyes came to the swinging double doors leading to the kitchen in which her brother Mathus was most likely cooking meals. At that thought, her stomach growled; it had been far too long since she last ate. Her eyes trailed back towards Sister Ranaa, going over the familiar details of the inn's interior. She had always loved this inn: the wooded floors, the soft wood-paneled walls that held up tapestries. There was one of Rockhide's family crest, and another with the familiar gauntleted hand of Torm, but her favorite tapestry was Tymora's. It displayed her face on a silver coin on a grass green back-drop. Finally she was eye to eye with Sister Ranaa, who had waited quietly for her to focus again.

Softly touching the shoulder that had not been bitten, Ranaa pulled her close. "There have been men in red robes asking questions of everyone for the past two days. Your mother and father have asked us to take you with us. They believe these men have ill intent towards the bards within the city."

Maddy became very focused when Sister Ranaa had said red robes, and was now twitching with anxiety. They had captured Maddy once with the pretext of questioning her about strange events in a city she stayed in. Maddy, however, was cuffed and taken to a holding cell in the dungeon. She had escaped, but had overheard a sinister voice telling the red-robed men to cut her tongue out. It wanted them to bring it to what Maddy assumed was a man. She had not been interested to see who or what it was, as she was far more concerned with getting herself as far away from these men as possible, and with her tongue right where it was. Her breath became shallow and she began to get a pit in her stomach.

"Grab what you can, we need to leave now. Even if I die from hunger, " she stated quickly, bolting for the stables and leaving Sister Ranaa behind. She gazed about, wondering what Maddy had been thinking as she looked around the place. To her it was just another inn, but clearly to Maddy it was more. When she exited the door towards the stable she found that Maddy had donned a plain burlap cloak, and was now sitting in the back of the cart with the hood pulled over her face. Ryan was helping Asuka with the last of the boxes of furs that Sister Ranaa had not had the time to sell in the market. When Ryan had jumped into the back of the cart himself, Maddy looked up.

"So, decided one look was not enough? Had to whisk away with me, did you?" Maddy said, looking over at Ryan with a sly smile, trying to hide her anxiety about the red men. Ryan ignored her, which made her sigh. He was more interested in the tome he was holding as he read it to himself with his finger sliding across the dry parchment. As she stared as his hand she noticed for the first time that parts of it were stained with ink. She decided to examine him closer. Ryan, though sitting, was clearly taller than Maddy by at least a head and a half. His dark hair was slightly curly, though Maddy could not tell if it was because of birth, or if he had simply not washed it. He wore a dark blue tunic with brown stitching. His leggings were black, and seemed stiff. His skin was slightly red, possibly from a long walk in the sun without a hood or hat. Maddy smirked- his clothes looked like they were washed far more often then he washed himself. His facial hair was dark as his regular hair, and was combed and tied off into a single length with what looked like a short strip of leather. His nose was slightly tilted towards the left as though it had had a bad break. Again Maddy thought to herself that, for a man, he was rather on the cute side. Much better than the muscled, fake "heroes" that harassed her at stops, trying to get private shows. It was one of the reasons that she posed as a man. Most men were pigs, and woman made better company anyway; they were far more subtle.

Maddy giggled, remembering the time she had lost a nice male top because a bunch of crazed young ladies had ripped her tunic to reveal her chest (which at the time was bound with bandages, as it was when she posed as male). She had escaped while they stood there stunned. Ryan looked up from his tome when he heard her giggle and looked at her, puzzled yet showing a soft redness on his cheeks that Maddy believed was not due to the sun.

Ranaa and Asuka had come around the cart and were now climbing into the driving area. With a small snap of the leather straps, the horse slowly started pulling the cart away. Just in time, it seemed, as men in red robes began walking down the dirt road the opposite direction, and were now going into the Merry Willow. Maddy watched as the swinging sign seemed to wave goodbye to her once again and fade into the rest of the city as they made their way to the gates.

The small brown horse clip-clopped his way through the city of people milling about, going about their lives. Maddy kept a searching eye out for men in red robes, without making it obvious. Her keen eyes saw what others did not. Men and woman who looked homeless in drab, unappealing clothing were making their ways through the city. Every so often they would stop someone to ask for spare copper. This was, in fact, the fleeing of bards, and of late it had become a necessary act. They were not actually looking for coppers, but playing the part. If they were lucky, they would be thrown out of the city by the guards.

Maddy heard a ruckus as the blacksmith growled at the red robes for harassing his customers. The guards at the closest gate had left their posts to settle the issue without violence. Meanwhile, several men and women walked out of the unattended gate and made on slowly, not wanting to pull attention to themselves.

Maddy sighed with relief and laid back when they had finally made it far into the fields west of Neverwinter. The snow made a soft crunching sound as both horse and cart went over it. The fields were always nice going through, even if they were out in the open. Now that they were finally home free Maddy's stomach had unknotted, and was once again free to complain about lack of food.

"Stupid red robes, now I don't get the breakfast I was promised," Maddy whined with her normal steadfastness. Asuka looked at her and handed her a brown parcel with a strip of parchment tied to it. Before opening it, Maddy unrolled the parchment and read it to herself.

**Dear Sister,

Sorry that you slept through your birthday, I know it meant a lot to you that mom was coming to visit. Because of that attack and the men in red robes we never got to have a sit down dinner. Well Mother, Father, and I did, but you were sorely missed as you slept in feverish dreams. Mom sends her best and wishes that you did not have to flee as she did. To make it up to you, I stayed up last night and made you this package. It holds a dozen honey cakes. Be good and share with your friends, they volunteered to take you away with them.

Love you,

Mathus***

Maddy after reading the letter kissed her coin and said a silent prayer for her family. She then tore into her package, and ate two of the apple filled honey cakes before offering some to the others. Asuka took one with a smile, Sister Ranaa waved it off, and Ryan took one and sniffed it before eating it very slowly. Maddy ate a fourth while watching Ryan pick up and put down the same one several times on to the clear space of the wooden planks they sat upon. He seemed really engrossed in the tome he was reading. Maddy was surprised that he was not getting an upset stomach from reading and the bumpy ride, let alone not losing his place. She cleared her throat and spoke softly, "How long have you been studying that magic tome?"

Ryan did not look up and at first Maddy thought he did not hear her she was about to speak up again when he said, "It is not a magic tome, nor is it a book of faith. It is my journal." With this, he simply went back to reading it. Maddy had heard of journals, a lot of bards she knew carried them, but she only knew them to write in them, not read them. Why would someone read a journal of a simple person's life, let alone their own?

Maddy turned her gaze to the slowly passing area. Snow was covering the rocky area they were passing through. What little grass grew in this area was hidden under three inches of snow. Maddy loved the snow; it brought forth fond memories and was her favorite part of growing up in Neverwinter. Saffera and Rockhide used to take them to the fields to play in the snow, because none would fall within the city itself. Maddy was rather good at tossing snowballs and would playfully pelt Mathus, who would eventually give up fighting back and go make strange men from the snow. They looked like sketches that she once saw in a tome called the Golem Manual.

Mathus had always been fascinated by the magical world, but he was too busy with his cooking to seriously pursue it. Maddy dabbled in magic, but like all bards her magic was more parlor tricks than the kind of magic that wizards do. Maddy found it humorous; for all their power, they could not heal wounds like she could. Not that she was anywhere as good as clerics.

They slowly passed over a wooden bridge that crossed a small ravine, which seemed to have widened as of late. The boards of the bridge creaked under the weight of cart and party but held strong. A small stream of water made from snowmelt was making a delightful noise that inspired Maddy to take out her harp. She began plucking out soft sweet notes when Sister Ranaa softly asked, "So who are the men in the red robes? Why are they hunting down bards?", continuing to watch the road as she listened for a reply.

Maddy hauled her playing and took in a slow deep breath of the cool air. "I do not know what they are called, but from what I gather, they are very powerful wizards. They are an organization that is supposed to monitor and prevent people from using too powerful of spells. Why they are hunting bards is beyond me, as we do not have access to powerful magic- unless you believe the legend of the Seeker of Songs." Maddy looked up to all eyes on her.

Ryan had even put his journal down and was looking at her, "Why would someone seek songs? Is it not a bard master's job to teach them?"

Maddy rolled her eyes at the fact that a scholar was asking her about history." A Seeker is not looking for common songs, they are looking for the primal songs: music that came about at the beginning of time, or even sooner, so the legend says. The songs are not mere noise or magically laced, they are the stuff of pure emotions. Word before word, sound before sound. It is said most cannot even comprehend what they have heard, but only feel the effects of the song," she continued, now standing and waving her hands for effect. She kneeled down and whispered into Ryan's ear, "to others, it is more pleasurable than bedding with one's true mate."

Maddy was very happy with herself when he hid his blushing face with his journal. "Mainly, they are bards who can project their very emotions into the world through music, and use elemental magic that rivals wizards." Maddy plucked at the strings some more, and recited from memory in time with the notes. "Rage brings fire to burn your foe, sadness floods the world with woe, calmness stills the harshest winds, and love makes the world shine anew."

Asuka and Ranaa clapped while Ryan stared in wonder. Maddy bowed, smiling, and raised a hand for silence. "However, as I said, they are just legends. The seeker tales are so rare because it was believed that only a single bloodline had the ability to achieve such a power. And we have to face the fact that if there is any with even a drop of that blood in them, they would still have to actually hear a song before they could come to possess it."

Asuka looked around at the snow and the hills in the distances. "You said that sadness floods the world with woe." Asuka turned around and looked at her. "Does that mean the bard could be so sad that it made the very skies cry?" Asuka turned back around and looked down like a child who felt that they had asked a stupid question.

Maddy patted her back and smiled at her with kindness, "I have heard how wood elves believe when it rains it is because the spirits of the sky weep. To answer your question, yes, it does mean make the sky rain, but it would be a fierce storm with winds howling with pain. And it would have to be a bard in such pain that their inner calmness was lost."

Sister Ranaa looked at Asuka with a lifted eyebrow and stated, "Maddy, that does sound like what happened the night of the attack. The bells were suddenly deafened by wind, and it sounded like someone was crying out in agony. The rain came, and it poured so hard that all of the fires were put out and the streets were partly flooded. No one else seemed to notice, but after the fires were out, the clouds dissipated instead of blowing away. "

Asuka looked up again and added with renewed confidence. "The wind howled but did not move the cloud, it was just there as though someone had willed it into being.

Asuka had stood up on the seat and it was starting to creak, so she quickly sat back down. She looked at Maddy, her face suddenly pale (or what looked like pale, with her darker complexion). "Maddy, are you a Seeker? Were the honey cakes that important to you?"

There was silence and everyone stared at her to the point that the horse stopped because Ranaa had pulled the reins to herself. Usually Maddy liked being the center of attention, but this was fear and not love. Putting her hands up carefully, she said, "One, that would be really shallow of me to get that upset over honey cakes," (though to herself she admitted that would not be too far off), "Two, the answer is simply, no, I am not a legendary, all-powerful bard."

To herself she remembered what the sinister voice said. Why did it want her tongue? Was this actually about seekers? She smiled through it to comfort her friends.

"I am just an attention-needing girl who found out a way to get attention, get free drinks, and get paid without doing something inappropriate." Maddy plucked a few more cords on her harp and smiled. She would not want to be a seeker anyway, she just wanted to live the good life, and she had learned early on you could do so more easily without power. If she was a seeker, she would probably get stuck doing some goodie god's dirty work with promises of love and remembrance after years of hard work. Oh yes, and death. The rewards of the afterlife in exchange for giving up the life you would have had if you just got a job and family. Not her idea of a fair trade.

"Enough about me, my stories grow stale. I want new things to think about, such as you and Asuka. " Maddy gestured encouragingly while plucking a soft melody to accompany the story. She noticed the sun was now halfway across the sky and Neverwinter could no longer be seen. They had made it to the wilderness.

Ranaa looked to Asuka and the shy wood elf nodded, "My life has been long, but the only thing eventful in it was meeting up with Sister Ranaa. It is not bard's tale." Maddy reassured her that not every story has to be an epic, and Asuka smiled and began while Maddy played the harp softly and dramaticly, to make the story more involving.

Sister Ranaa had been born into a noble high elven family, and on her one hundredth anniversary of life was given Asuka as a servant. Sister Ranaa had protested having a servant, as it was unbecoming to her, but she was not given a choice. As time passed she had become very fond of Asuka, who had admitted that she enjoyed doing things for her. When Ranaa turned 120 years of age, she had become a well known druid among her people thanks to Asuka's help. Ranaa became Sister Ranaa and was allowed to venture out of the city to begin her life as an adult.

However, the world was much crueler then the elven village where she had grown up. Her career as a druid was not making much money, as those who came to her for healing and treatment only did so because they were too poor to pay for treatment at the temples.

Even though she gathered her own herbs, she was still not making enough to feed her and Asuka. Luckily, Asuka had been a great hunter when still living with her people, even at the young age of 55.

With the little money Ranaa had saved up, she bought a sling to attempt to hunt, unaware that Asuka could do so. Asuka had embraced her, taken the sling, and run off. Sister Ranaa felt abandoned, and lost to the world. She fled to the inn room they had bought, and wept in her pillow till she fell asleep.

She awoke the next morning to a very tired Asuka resting at her feet. There was a line of three hares hanging from their feet. Her Asuka had not abandoned her, but instead had mistaken Sister Ranaa's buying of the sling as a gift for her to hunt for their food. After selling a few nicely made hare and snake leather they had enough to buy a bow and some arrows. Thus they began their career of selling leather and dry meats across the land of Faerun.

Their victory over life's misfortunes had a bitter sweetness, as, even selling the leathers, most merchants still refused to buy from woman, or pay as much for their product as they would have a man's. Sister Ranaa had been arrested once for breaking a merchant's nose when he had suggested he pay top dollar for her slave girl when Asuka had called Ranaa Mistress.

With a grin, Asuka stopped telling their story and looked at Maddy hopefully. Maddy stopped plucking her strings and gave a small round of claps. "See there, all you need is a little music and you tell like a natural bard." Asuka blushed at such a nice complement. Maddy laid her head back and watched the sky darken while returning to softly playing her harp.

The ground had grown softer the further they traveled south, away from her mountain home, and the day was growing colder with the dark. Trees were more abundant in these lower grounds, and the scenery was finally worth looking at. Tall trees reached for the sky and small bushes were scattered as though their seeds had been planted by someone dancing a ballet. The road they travelled was like a scar on the body of the land, barren and dark compared to the white and green around them.

Sister Ranaa was looking to either side of the road for a nice clearing. When she saw one, she urged her horse to the left of the road with a gentle tug on the reins. Maddy looked up and saw an area where the grass was poking out of the thin layer of snow and was surrounded at a distance by a line of trees. In the middle of the clearing was a set of stones in the shape of a circle. The stones showed black smudges from a previous fire; however, the same layer of snow lay inside the circle, so it had not been recent. No tracks were in the snow other than their own. Sister Ranaa looked to Maddy with the silent question.

Maddy looked into the trees and back towards the road. "I will take the first watch and gather firewood. You two set up the tents and get some rest." Maddy headed back to the cart and grabbed the ax from the back of it. "Ryan, is it? Why don't you help me carry the wood so that I don't have to put it down at each stop."

Without waiting for an answer, Maddy walked off. Ryan put his journal away in his pack and followed after jumping out of the cart and landed running after her.

"You do not have to tell me what to do, I am willing to help after all." Maddy was ignoring him, looking around the trees until she came to a fallen one and began swinging the ax slowly at it, cutting pieces of wood from it. "Why have we come out this far for a dead tree? There were plenty alive back there, closer to the camp." Maddy continued to chop wood and hand the bits to him, ignoring him as she wiped her brow.

Maddy dropped a large piece of wood in his waiting hands and as he started swaying from the weight she steadied him and whispered into his ear, not looking at him, "We're not in your little monastery here, Scholar, this is the wilderness and people are not nice. Do you not realize how lucky it is that we found a fire pit in this clearing?" Maddy's emphasis on the word 'lucky' was clearly sarcastic.

She began walking him towards the campsite again. "I came out this far, not searching for wood, but for tracks. I do not need you to carry the wood, it was just an excuse to have backup. Taking Asuka would have left Sister Ranaa defenseless." Ryan did not give any sign of understanding, or even acknowledgment that she had said anything to him. Maddy was glad that he was not as thickheaded as most of the males she had met.

Maddy said loudly, "You complain too much, what have I told you? If the goddess provides you with a dead tree, then cut it. Dead wood burns faster and hotter than living wood does."

Ryan rolled his eyes. "Yeah, like you saw the tree from this far away, you're so full of it." They walked back to the campsite with the wood, making small talk so that they could hear if someone was around without letting them know. When they got to the campsite, the tents were up and ready to be slept in. If any sleep was to be done. Maddy was dismayed at the two tents: she knew better then to ask that Asuka or Ranaa sleep in the other tent with Ryan.

Asuka started a small fire using the wood cut by Maddy, and slowly roasted a few fish that she had gotten from a nearby creek. Along with the fish they had some slightly stale rye bread and some bitter tasting turnips that were past their prime. It was still better then what Maddy had to eat on the road normally. Sister Ranaa and Asuka retired to their tent, and laid down on warm furs that they kept for themselves. Maddy had told them that she needed no comforts and Ryan did not want to impose.

"I have heard their story, and I am sure that since they brought you along, they have heard yours." Maddy picked up her harp and smiled as she plucked at the cords. "Now it is time you told me yours, and do not even think of just handing me that journal of yours."

Ryan sat back against the tree and looked into the fire. "Where to begin... I guess with the story I was writing." Ryan told Maddy that he was in the middle of writing a fantastic story. A hero so purely good that all the gods, evil and good, smiled upon him. A man whom could do no wrong. Unfortunately, as he was finishing his epic tale, the headmaster of the monastery had walked in and seen the book of faith that he was supposed to be copying closed on his desk. The head master grabbed the book that Ryan was writing in and, after reading the first line, threw the book into the fire. The headmaster dragged him by the ear to a room that was meant for punishment. The walls were gray and the ceiling high and windowless. When the door was closed, you were trapped in compete darkness. Before he shut the door, he told Ryan that this was fate of liars in the afterlife, no matter their intentions.

Ryan did not know how long he had been there, for how does one tell time when there is no light to break the night? What he did know was that he was starving and had become quite pungent when they finally opened the door again. The headmaster had thought Ryan would have learned, but all Ryan learned was to hide it till someone could appreciate it.

A friend of his found him in time to tell him that the headmaster was looking for him because of a tome. Ryan had run away from the monastery, leaving the completed work in the hands of the headmaster.

He had planned to rewrite the story, but had come to find that the real world was corrupt, no matter who claimed to be a hero. In truth, he saw that they were not valor-filled, but instead treasure-crazed, murderous men who only appeared to be good because they killed beings that were not the same as those they claimed to protect.

That was when he realized that people who got jobs and raised families were far more valorous then these so-called "heroes".

He had walked in to the attack of the city from those vile, black-furred, orc-like creatures, and was inspired by a woman who had attacked the creature, not to kill it, but to save a little girl. One who did not desire to be thanked, but only to save her village. After this new heroine had saved the village, using the bell to warn them, she had been brought to the medical tents for an infected wound.

He had gone around town asking about her. Ryan stopped his story to look at Maddy with judgmental eyes. "They told me that she was a drunk who flew in and out of town with the troubles and was as much a nuisance as a hero." Maddy shrugged. Admittedly, she did have a big mouth, and enjoyed showing off a bit. "However, I have decided that not every hero is perfect, or even a hero at all. Sometimes, they are just good people. So that is what is in the journal. An account of my time reflecting my values, because some drunken tease is more of a hero than any man I ever met."

Before Maddy could respond, there was the crunch of boots on snow. Five men stood at the other end of the fire, grinning, with malice in their dark eyes. Maddy reached into the bag in front of her and pulled out her harp. The men approached, the crunch of snow beneath their feet the only sound before she started to play. A soothing tune came and one of the men yawned greatly scratched his belly and layed down in the snow the other four followed suit shortly after. Ryan felt a hand grab him and shake him he woke up face down in the snow and turned over to see Maddy offering him a water skin. He drowsing drank from it. Whatever it was it tasted bitter with hints of sweet cream. His eyes opened more easily and stood up.

"What just happened did one of the bandits get the drop on me." Ryan asked checking his head while brushing snow off himself.

Maddy smiled and laughed a little, "Sorry sometimes the spell is a bit too strong. Old bard trick for getting out of trouble is to play a lullaby. Bonus is these guys will wake up eventually feeling like they just had a best sleep in their lives now help me tie them up." Maddy explained as she got out the lengths of rope and bound the bandits hands.

Ryan looked them over and sighed, "Were on the run what do we do with them." Ryan began to pace as he considered.

"What other choice do we have leave them in my tent with a knife and they will escape after were miles away from here." Maddy replied throwing her hands up. "What I do know is that the world is in grave danger if they are hunting bards than they must be after seekers of the songs. Which means some egomaniac is after the final Requiem."

Ryan turns with a lifted eye brow. "What would anyone hunt bards to get a song meant to be sung at a funereal?"

"The Final Requiem when played will kill everything that hears it. Legend says it is only heard by those who die in a natural disaster." Maddy answers her eyes taking on an ethereal light as though she is not the one speaking.

Printed in Great Britain
by Amazon